# Big Brown Bear
# Goes to Town

Harcourt, Inc.

ORLANDO   AUSTIN   NEW YORK
SAN DIEGO   TORONTO   LONDON

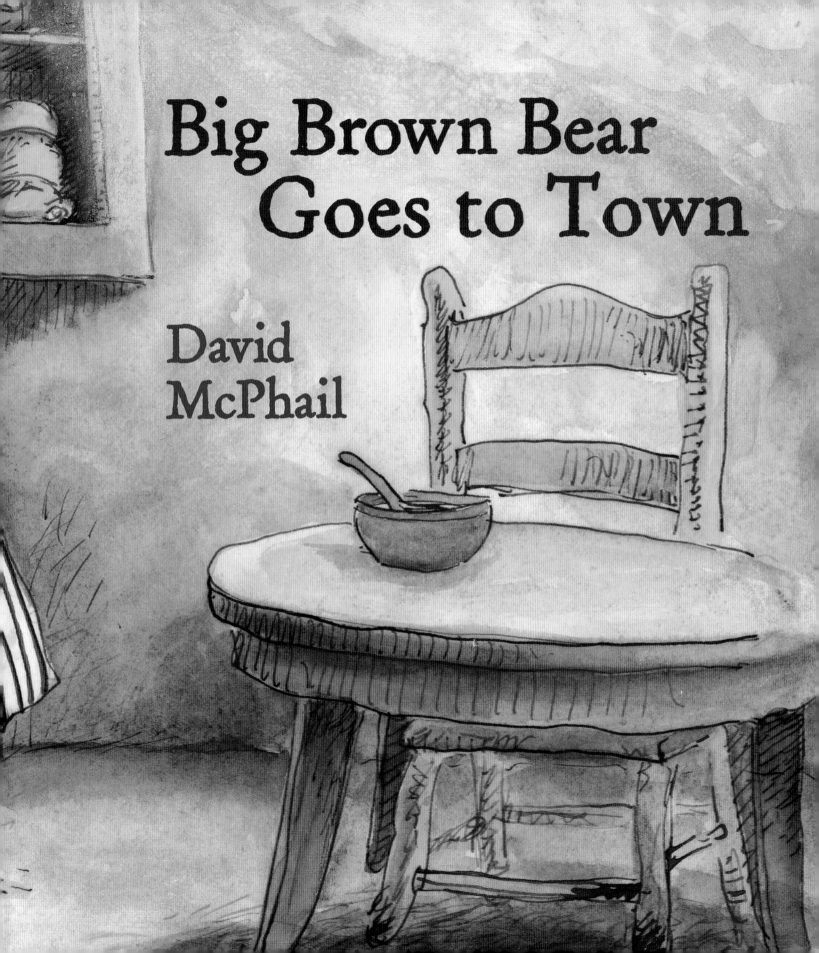

# Big Brown Bear Goes to Town

## David McPhail

www.HarcourtBooks.com

Library of Congress Cataloging-in-Publication Data
McPhail, David, 1940–
Big Brown Bear goes to town/David McPhail.
p.   cm.
Summary: Rat's car fills up with water when it rains, but his friend Big Brown Bear comes to the rescue.
[1. Friendship—Fiction.   2. Rain and rainfall—Fiction.   3. Bears—Fiction.   4. Rats—Fiction.]
I. Title.
PZ7.M4788184Big   2006
[E]—dc22      2005009955
ISBN-13: 978-0152-05317-8   ISBN-10: 0-15-205317-4

First edition

H G F E D C B A

Printed in Singapore

The illustrations in this book were done in pen and ink and watercolor.
The display type and text type were set in Old Claude.
Color separations by Bright Arts Ltd., Hong Kong
Printed and bound by Tien Wah Press, Singapore
This book was printed on totally chlorine-free Stora Enso Matte paper.
Production supervision by Ginger Boyer
Designed by Lauren Rille

For Stephen and August,
and for their father, Peter, the Snowplow Man

# One

While Big Brown Bear waited for his oatmeal to cool, he went out to get the mail.

It must have rained in the night, because there were puddles everywhere. But the letters inside the mailbox were as dry as a bone.

"What a good mailbox I have," declared Big Brown Bear. "No matter how hard it rains, the mail never gets wet."

He was walking back up the path to his house when he noticed that his friend Rat's little yellow car had filled with rainwater. Big Brown Bear picked up the car, emptied it, and put it back down.

Just then, Rat appeared. He was carrying a bucket.

"What's the bucket for, Rat?" Big Brown Bear asked.

"Every time it rains, my car fills with water," replied Rat. "I use the bucket to bail it out."

"Too late," chuckled Big Brown Bear. "I already took care of it."

"Thank you," said Rat.
"You saved me a lot of time and hard work."

"I'm glad to help," said Bear.
"But why don't you bring the car
inside when it rains?"

"It won't fit through my
doorway," explained Rat.
"If only I had a nice dry
place to keep it."

"Yes, that would be
good," agreed Bear.
And then he had an idea.

"I'm going to town now,"
Rat told Bear. "Would you like
to come with me?"

"Yes, I would," replied Bear.
"There is something I want to get."

So, Rat started up the car, and off to town they went.

# Two

"Where do you want to go?" asked Rat.

"I want to go to the hardware store," said Big Brown Bear, "but first I need to stop at the bank."

"The bank it is, then," Rat shouted over the wind.

When they arrived at the bank,
Rat steered the car right through
the door. He screeched to a halt
at the teller's window.

"May I help you?" the teller asked.

"I would like some money," said Big Brown Bear.

"And how much would you like?" the teller inquired pleasantly.

"Enough to buy something at the hardware store," explained Big Brown Bear. Then he leaned forward and whispered to the teller so that Rat couldn't hear.

The teller counted out some money and handed it to Big Brown Bear.

"Now, to the hardware store, Rat,"
said Big Brown Bear, "if you please."
And off they zoomed.

# Three

When they got to the hardware store, Big Brown Bear jumped off the car and dashed inside. "I'll be right out," he called to Rat.

"And I'll be right back," Rat replied.

Rat was waiting when Big Brown Bear
came out of the hardware store carrying a box.
"What's in the box, Bear?" asked Rat.
"You'll see soon enough," Big Brown Bear replied.

"You've been awfully secretive today, Bear," said Rat, "and did you know that whispering is rude?"

"I'm sorry, Rat," said Big Brown Bear. "I certainly didn't mean to be rude."

"Oh, it is no big deal," said Rat. "It's just not like you, is all."

"Maybe when we get home things will explain themselves," said Big Brown Bear.

"Home, then," said Rat,
and in no time at all they were there.

# Four

"Now, please close your eyes, Rat," said Big Brown Bear, "and don't open them until I tell you to."

As Rat waited, he heard the sound of a box being torn open. Then he heard the sound of metal creaking.

"Okay, Rat," cried Big Brown Bear, "now you can look!"

When Rat looked he saw that his shiny yellow car was missing. In its place was a . . . What was it, anyway?

It was a mailbox! Just like the one that stood on a post in front of Big Brown Bear's house. "What do you think, Rat?" asked Big Brown Bear excitedly.

"It's a beauty, Bear," answered the somewhat bewildered Rat. "But honestly, I don't need something that big. I don't get a lot of mail, you know."

Big Brown Bear smiled.

"It's not for your mail," he said.

"It's for your car!"

Then he opened the door to reveal the little yellow car sitting snugly and securely inside.

"Oh, Bear," cried Rat, "it's brilliant! Now my car has a nice dry house of its own."

"Yes indeed, Rat," said Big Brown Bear, as drops of rain from a passing shower started to fall. "Now do you mind telling me what *your* errand was?"

Rat went inside and came
back with a large sack.
"I went to get brown sugar,"
he explained, "for my oatmeal."

"Marvelous!" said Bear. "It just so happens that I made some oatmeal this morning. I imagine it's cool enough to eat by now."

And sure enough . . .

. . . it was.